The Fooling of King Alexander

BY MERVYN SKIPPER

ILLUSTRATED BY GAYNOR CHAPMAN

ATHENEUM   New York   *1967*

Alexander was a very great king. The Kings of Persia, Media, India, and Brunei are all descended from him. He conquered Stamboul, Mesopotamia, Bombay, and Singapore, and when he had conquered all these he thought

3

he had conquered all the world; but one day he met an
old woman washing rice in a river, and he spoke to her

about it. "No," said the old woman, "there is still one country left to conquer. You have not conquered China."

"Where is this China?" asked Alexander.

"It lies beyond the great snow mountains, the deserts of sliding sands, the land of two-headed men, beyond the

jungle of knives and scissors, the land where geese grow on trees, the land of legless people who go about on wheels, the country of tongueless women, and the ocean of flying whales."

"And how far is that?" asked Alexander.

"Just how far that is, my lord," said the old woman, "nobody knows."

"However far away it is," said Alexander, "I will conquer

it." And he ordered all his army to be got together, his
hundreds of elephants, his thousands of camels, his tens
of thousands of horses, and of foot-soldiers and their
wives and children, thousands without number; and at

the head of these he set out to conquer China. Such was
the size of his army that the jungle of knives and scissors
was trampled flat, the snow mountains nodded their heads
till their snow caps fell off and ran down into the valleys,
the sliding sands rose in clouds and obscured the sun and

made the day so dark that if it had not been for the
glittering of the swords and shields, and the crowns
of the rajas, nobody would have been able to see his way.
When it thundered, the thunder could not be heard for
the shouting of the foot-soldiers, the neighing of the

horses, and the trumpeting of the elephants; and the very swiftest camels were required if one wished to go from

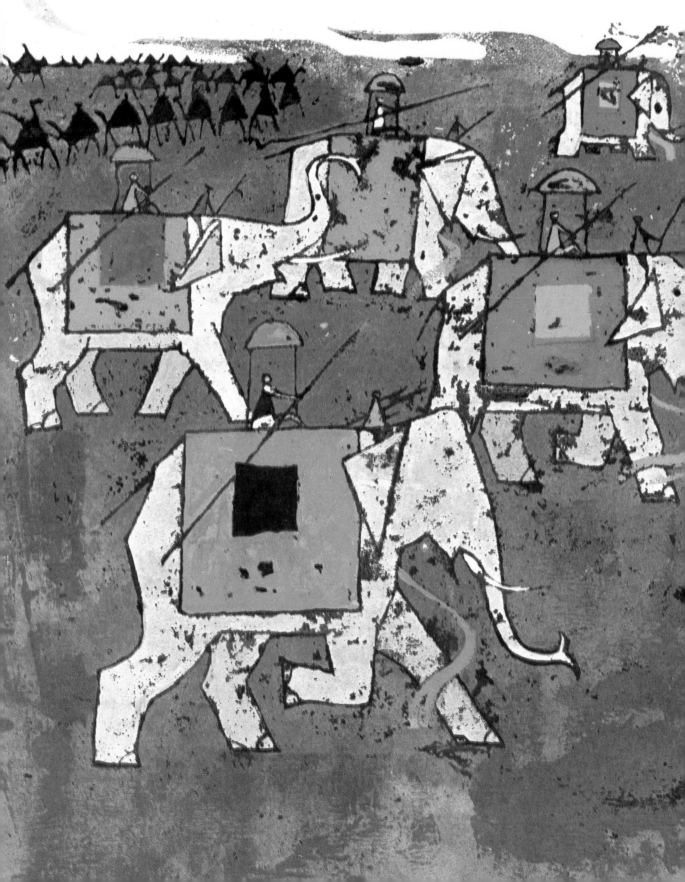

the head of the army to the tail of it between
breakfast-time and dinner. It was a very great

army. For many days King Alexander marched, and at

last he came to Temasek, which is not far from China.

Now, when the Emperor of China heard that King Alexander was coming to take his country from him with this great army, he was frightened and his liver turned to water. Calling all his wisest men together, he asked what

was the best thing to be done.
Some said one thing and
some said another, and they
all talked at once and made a
great noise; but none of them
could tell the Emperor how he
could stop King Alexander
and his soldiers from taking
China. At last, when they had
all got tired of talking, the
little boy who carried the
Emperor's snuff-box stood out
and said he knew a way to
stop King Alexander. The
wise men laughed, but the
Emperor said: "Let the boy
speak! A small stone can
sometimes break a large jar!"

So the little boy asked the
Emperor to give him the oldest and rottenest junk

that he had in his navy; and he had it filled right up
to the decks with small and rusty needles. Then he took

a kesma tree and a jujube
tree that were in fruit and
planted them in tubs on the
deck. Then he asked the Emperor to give him for his crew
six old men whose teeth had
all dropped out, and six old
women whose backs were bent

like water-wheels, to keep them company. So the Emperor sent his messengers out to find six old men whose teeth had all dropped out, and six old women whose backs were bent like water-wheels, and when they were found

they were put on board the junk, the small boy took the tiller, and the junk set out towards Temasek.

The wise men laughed when they saw the junk go; but the Emperor said, "Wait and see: beards sometimes grow before eyebrows."

After a few days the junk came to Temasek, and when King Alexander's army saw it they ran to the King, crying that a junk had arrived that had come from China.

"Go, fools," said King Alexander, "and ask the crew of the junk how far they have come and how far it is to China."

"Alas," said the crew of the junk, "the day that we set sail from China we were all young men and beautiful women, twelve years was the age of the oldest of us. These fruit-bearing trees, we planted them as seeds. Now, alas! we are old, and our teeth have fallen

out, and our backs have become bent like water-wheels, and the seeds have grown into great trees, and at last we have come to this place."

And they showed their cargo of needles to King Alexander's men, and said, "As big and round as our arms were these bars of iron when we left China; see how they have rusted to the size of needles; that is how long our journey has been so that we forget the number of the years of it; and if the small boy who steers had not been born to us ten years ago there would have been none left strong enough to sail the vessel."

So King Alexander's people went to King Alexander and told him all that the crew of the junk had told them.

"If, as these Chinese say, this country of China is so far away that boys grow into old men on the journey, how should I ever be able to reach it since I am already an old man?" said King Alexander.

"True, O King!" cried all his people. "Let us return!"

And so King Alexander and all his army returned to their own country. And when they came to the river from whence they had started, the old woman was still washing rice in it.

As for the boy, the one who had carried the snuff-box of the Emperor and sailed the junk to Temasek, he sailed back to China. And when the Emperor heard what had been done, he was well satisfied. "Truly," he said, "wisdom is not always with the wise. Come boy, there is much yet for you to do."

THE LEGEND
OF THE
CHRISTMAS
ROSE

SELMA LAGERLÖF

THE LEGEND OF THE CHRISTMAS ROSE

retold by
ELLIN GREENE
with illustrations by
CHARLES MIKOLAYCAK

HOLIDAY HOUSE
New York

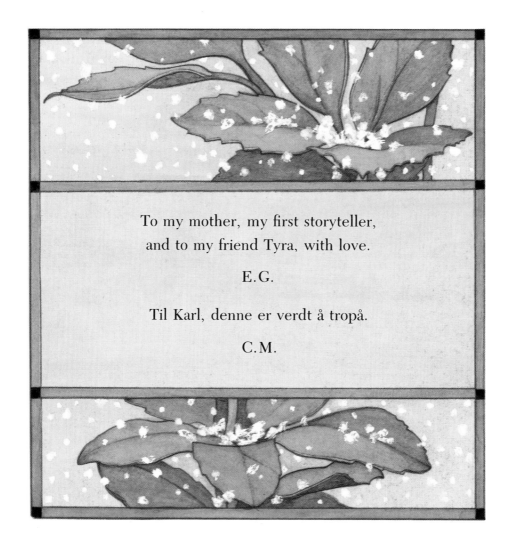

To my mother, my first storyteller,
and to my friend Tyra, with love.

E.G.

Til Karl, denne er verdt å tropå.

C.M.

Rᴏʙʙᴇʀ Mᴏᴛʜᴇʀ, ᴡʜᴏ ʟɪᴠᴇᴅ ɪɴ Rᴏʙʙᴇʀs' Cᴀᴠᴇ ᴜᴘ ɪɴ Göɪɴɢᴇ Forest with Robber Father and their five children, went down to the village one day to beg. Robber Father did not go with her.

Years before, Robber Father had been caught stealing a neighbor's cow, and the bishop had outlawed him, threatening to put him in prison if he ever dared to show his face in the village again. But sometimes, when food was scarce or the children's clothing had worn to tatters, Robber Mother would take all five youngsters into the village to beg. When the villagers saw Robber Mother and her wild-looking brood coming down the road, they would quickly put a bundle of used clothing or a parcel of food on their doorstep and bolt their doors. No one spoke kindly to Robber Mother and her children or invited them indoors, even in the coldest weather.

On this particular day, when Robber Mother and her children were out begging, they happened to pass Ovid Cloister. The cloister was situated in a beautiful park east of the lake. The grounds were surrounded by a stone wall, but today the gate was ajar and the youngest of the Robber children scampered in. In a moment she was back, tugging at her mother's skirt and pulling her toward the open gate.

When Robber Mother entered the grounds, she found herself standing at the foot of a magnificent garden laid out in the shape of a cross. The corners of the flower beds had been rounded and a giant fountain had been set in the center of the intersecting paths. Each section of the cross had been planted with a different variety of flowers—sweetly-scented roses; rosemary, rue, and other healing herbs; brilliantly colored lilies; and exotic plants. Robber Mother's stern look softened into an indulgent smile. Holding her youngest by the hand, she began walking along the stone-paved path toward the fountain. The other Robber children followed close behind.

When the lay brother who was tending the garden saw Robber Mother with all five youngsters in tow, he shouted for them to leave at once. "This is the abbot's private garden," he said, "and you have no right to be here." Robber Mother's smile changed to a scowl so fierce that it sent the lay brother reeling backwards. "I am Robber Mother from Göinge Forest," she answered sharply, "so touch me if you dare! I will leave when I have finished looking."

At this the lay brother became greatly agitated since

women were not allowed in the monastery, and it was he who had left the gate open. "If you don't leave, the monks will be angry with me for forgetting to close the gate and may send me away," he pleaded. But Robber Mother paid no more attention to his pleas than to his shouts and continued walking toward the fountain.

The lay brother decided there was nothing to be done but to run to the cloister and ask for help. He returned with two monks. The monks tried to persuade Robber Mother to leave, and when she refused, they each took her by an arm and turned her toward the gate. Robber Mother planted her feet firmly on the path and began to shriek in a hoarse, strident voice. At the same time, the children threw themselves on the monks, biting and kicking. They caused such an uproar that the old abbot himself came out to see what was the matter.

The lay brother explained that Robber Mother and her children had invaded the garden and now refused to leave. The abbot scolded the monks for trying to use force and sent them back to the cloister. "Get on with your work," he ordered the lay brother. "I will see to this matter."

Meanwhile, Robber Mother had gone back to wandering among the flower beds. The abbot, certain that the woman had never seen such a splendid garden, was surprised to find her so at home. He greeted her gently and asked if the garden pleased her.

Robber Mother was expecting a different sort of welcome and now, when she looked at the abbot and noticed his white hair and frail frame, her anger left her. "It is a fine garden," she replied, "but it cannot be compared with another that I know."

The garden was the one earthly thing about which the abbot was vain. He had spent long hours cultivating his plants, many of them brought to him by sea captains who traveled to faraway lands. Robber Mother's words offended the good monk, and he replied coldly that he was not familiar with the garden of which she spoke.

"I tell you the truth," Robber Mother cried in a loud voice, her face growing crimson with rage. "You who are holy men surely ought to know that once a year on Christmas Eve a part of Göinge Forest is transformed into a beautiful garden in remembrance of the birthday of the Christ Child. And in that garden I have seen flowers far more lovely than any here."

At this the lay brother gave a scornful laugh. "The abbot has gathered plants from far and near, and there is not a lovelier garden to be found in all of Sweden."

But the abbot's heart stirred with memories of stories heard in childhood. He longed to see the Christmas garden and begged Robber Mother to send one of her children on Christmas Eve to show him the way.

At first Robber Mother refused, fearing that the abbot would betray the Robbers' hiding place. But the abbot

promised he would do the Robber family no harm and even offered, in return for her kindness, to ask the bishop to grant Robber Father a pardon. In the end, Robber Mother agreed to send her eldest son on Christmas Eve to guide the old abbot through the forest. "But mind that you bring only the lay brother with you," she warned. The abbot promised, and Robber Mother went on her way.

In the autumn the bishop visited the cloister. While the two men were walking in the garden, the abbot related the story of Robber Mother's visit and the Christmas garden. "Will you not give Robber Father a pardon so that the Robber family may once more live in the village? If God allows him to see a miracle, there must be some good in the man. Surely it would be better for his children to live among the villagers than to grow up as outlaws."

The bishop smiled at the old man's simple faith. "On the day that you send me a flower from the Christmas garden," he said, "I will pardon Robber Father." The abbot thanked the bishop for his promise and said that he would send him the flower next Christmas Day.

Christmas Eve came at last. The abbot packed a parcel of food, a bottle of wine, and sweets for the Robber children. Then he and the lay brother walked through the village to the edge of Göinge Forest, where the eldest Robber son waited for them.

The abbot had set forth joyously, but the lay brother was not at all happy to be going on what seemed to him a pointless journey. He did not believe Robber Mother's story about a garden that bloomed in winter, but he was too fond of the frail old monk to refuse to accompany him. He longed for the warmth of the cloister hearth and the smell of goose roasting for the Christmas feast.

Robber Son led them through the dense forest. Sometimes the path was steep and the horses stumbled. Sometimes the lay brother had to dismount to guide them over fallen trees covered with snow. The farther they went, the colder it grew. The lay brother fretted and grumbled, but the abbot's thoughts were on the miracle he was about to witness. As the sun's rays began to weaken, they came to a forest meadow. Beyond the meadow loomed a mountain wall, and cut into the wall was a door made of thick wooden planks. Robber Son pulled back the heavy door. Inside the mountain grotto Robber Mother was seated beside a log fire that burned in the middle of the floor. Robber Father was taking a nap. The four younger Robber children were sprawled on the floor around a large pot of watery gruel. There were no signs of Christmas celebration here!

"Sit by the fire and warm yourself, Father Abbot," Robber Mother greeted him. "And if you are tired from your long journey, sleep awhile for I will wake you when it is time to see what you have come all this way to see."

The abbot thanked Robber Mother, stretched out on a pile of dried bracken beside the fire, and soon fell into a deep sleep.

The lay brother was also invited to rest, but he refused, thinking he had better keep an eye on Robber Father. Gradually, fatigue got the better of him and he, too, dozed off.

When he awoke he saw that the abbot had left his bed and was talking with Robber Mother by the fire. Robber Father sat nearby with his back to them, as though he were not interested in their conversation.

The abbot was describing the Christmas preparations taking place in the village. Robber Mother listened intently, remembering the Christmas celebrations of her youth. Suddenly, her husband turned and shook his fist in the abbot's face. "No more of this talk! Have you come to coax from me my wife and children? Don't you know that I am an outlaw and may not enter the village?"

The abbot spoke calmly. "It is my purpose to get a letter of pardon for you from the bishop." At his words, Robber Father burst out laughing—he knew well enough the kind of mercy a forest robber could expect from the bishop!

Before the abbot could tell him about the bishop's promise, their conversation was interrupted by the sound of church bells ringing in Christmas. The abbot rose and followed the Robber family to the entrance of the cave.

The forest was as dark as before but instead of an icy

wind, a gentle breeze stirred from the south. The church bells stopped ringing, and in the stillness the winter darkness turned to the pale pinks of dawn. The snow vanished from the ground, the moss-turf thickened and raised itself, and the spring blossoms shot their pale-colored buds upward. The ferns unfolded their fronds that had been curled like a bishop's staff. The trees burst into leaf as suddenly as if a thousand green butterflies had lit in their branches. A pair of finches began building a nest. Baby squirrels played tag among the branches. A mother fox came out of her lair and proudly paraded her young past Robber Mother. The air was filled with birdsong and the lazy droning of bees. It seemed to the abbot that the angels themselves were singing.

Wave upon wave of light pulsed through the forest. A strong south wind scattered meadow seeds from southern lands over the forest. The seeds took root and sprang up the instant they touched the ground.

Robber Mother and Father stood transfixed, but the Robber children shrieked with delight. They gamboled in the soft grass, stuffed their mouths full of raspberries, and picked armfuls of wild flowers.

The abbot bent to pluck a wild strawberry blossom and, as he straightened up, the berry ripened in his hand. Everything was changing so rapidly that he did not have time to think of each wonder that happened. He thought of the flower he was to send to the bishop, but

each new flower that appeared seemed more beautiful than the last one, and he wanted to choose the most beautiful of all.

The abbot's heart trembled with joy that he had been allowed to witness such a miracle, but the mind of the lay brother was filled with dark thoughts. He knew that no matter how hard he might work with hoe and spade, he could never bring forth such a garden. "This cannot be a true miracle since it is revealed to outlaws," he thought to himself. "It must be the work of the Evil One performed to delude us!"

All this time the birds circled around the abbot's head or rested in his hands. But they were afraid of the lay brother. No bird perched on his shoulder.

Then a little forest dove plucked up courage, flew down to the lay brother's shoulder, and laid her head against his cheek. Frightened out of his wits and thinking that the devil had come upon him, the lay brother struck the forest dove with his hand and cried in such a loud voice that it rang throughout the forest, "Go thou back to Hell from whence thou art come!"

At the sound of his words, the angels' song was hushed for the darkness in a human heart. The light and warmth vanished. Darkness sank over the earth like a coverlet, all the flowers shriveled up, the leaves fell from the trees, and the birds and animals fled. An icy wind covered the earth and trees with snow. The Robber family and the lay

brother ran shivering back to the cave. But the abbot did not move. A cold anguish seized his heart as he realized what was happening. The abbot stumbled forward and at the same moment, remembering the flower he was to deliver to the bishop, clutched a handful of earth as he fell.

When the abbot did not return to the cave, the lay brother went out to look for him and found him dead under a blanket of snow. Lifting the old monk gently, he carried him back to the cloister. There the abbot was laid to rest, a radiant smile on his face.

The monks found a pair of root bulbs in the abbot's clutched hand and gave them to the lay brother. The lay brother planted them in the abbot's garden and tended them with great care. All through the spring, the summer, and the autumn, he waited in vain for the roots to send up shoots. When winter settled in, he gave up hoping that the bulbs would ever flower. But when Christmas Eve came again, he was so reminded of the abbot that he wandered into the garden to think of him. And when he came to the spot where he had planted the roots, he was astonished to see a cluster of flowers with silvery white petals and pale golden stamens. He had seen the flowers only once before—on Christmas Eve in the garden at Göinge Forest.

Taking a few blossoms to the bishop, he said, "The

abbot sends you a flower from the Christmas garden, as he promised." Then he told the bishop all that had happened that Christmas Eve. The bishop had long ago forgotten the abbot's promise, for he thought it was only an old man's dream. When the lay brother had finished speaking, the bishop sat thinking of his own promise to the abbot. "The abbot has faithfully kept his word, and I shall keep mine," he said. He wrote out a pardon for Robber Father and gave it to the lay brother to deliver. The lay brother departed at once for Robbers' Cave.

When he reached the clearing, Robber Father saw him coming and shouted at him to go away. "Thanks to you, we have had no Christmas garden this year," he raged.

"What you say is true, Robber Father. The fault is mine alone and I would gladly die for it. But first I must deliver your pardon from the bishop. You are free to return to the village to live among your people, as the good abbot promised you."

And so the Robber family returned to the village, where they lived in harmony with their neighbors and celebrated many Christmases together.

The lay brother did not return to the cloister. He chose to stay in Robbers' Cave and live a life of meditation and prayer, hoping that his hard-heartedness might be forgiven him.

The Christmas garden never again bloomed in Göinge Forest. But each year at Christmas time the plant that the abbot plucked from the garden sends forth its green stalks and white blossoms in celebration of the birthday of the Christ Child.

It is called the Christmas Rose.

❋

AUTHOR'S NOTE

THERE ARE SEVERAL LEGENDS THAT EXPLAIN THE ORIGIN OF THE Christmas Rose. This retelling is adapted from Selma Lagerlöf's *The Legend of the Christmas Rose*, published in *Good Housekeeping* December 1907. Ms. Lagerlöf is best known to children for her books, *The Wonderful Adventures of Nils* and *The Further Adventures of Nils* in which she combined the folklore, history, and geography of Sweden. Sweden's annual children's book prize is named the Nils Hölgersson Award after Lagerlöf's fictional hero. Ms. Lagerlöf had a lifelong interest in Swedish folklore fostered by her grandmother's retellings of local legends and tales. In 1909 this gifted storyteller became the first woman to receive the Nobel Prize for Literature.

The Christmas Rose (*Helleborus niger*) is not really a rose. It is a member of the buttercup family. The pale white flower seems to rise miraculously from the cold wintry earth, serving to remind us that life is full of miracles.

Ellin Greene,
May 15, 1989

Library of Congress Cataloging-in-Publication Data
Greene, Ellin,
The legend of the Christmas rose / written by Selma Lagerlöf ;
retold by Ellin Greene ; illustrated by Charles Mikolaycak.

p.   cm.
Translation of: Legenden om julrosorna.
Summary: In hope of getting her husband pardoned,
an exiled outlaw's wife agrees to reveal to an old monk
the miracle in Goinge Forest, where every Christmas Eve
a beautiful garden blooms in remembrance
of the birth of the Christ Child.
ISBN 0-8234-0821-3
[1. Folklore—Sweden.   2. Christmas—Folklore.]
I. Mikolaycak, Charles, ill.   II. Lagerlöf, Selma, 1858-1940.
Legenden om julrosorna.   III. Title.
PZ8.1.G785 Le 1990
398.21'09485—dc20   [E]   89-77511   CIP   AC

Designed by Charles Mikolaycak

Thanks to Dad, Dag, Gwen and Chris.   C.M.